THE PREGNANT VIRGIN

THE PREGNANT VIRGIN

How come?

A Novel

Divine M. Chiangeh

iUniverse, Inc.

New York Lincoln Shanghai

The Pregnant Virgin

How come?

iUniverse books may be ordered through booksellers or by contacting:

iUniverse
2021 Pine Lake Road, Suite 100
Lincoln, NE 68512
www.iuniverse.com
1-800-Authors (1-800-288-4677)

This is a work of fiction. All of the characters, names, incidents, organizations and dialogue in this novel are either the products of the author's imagination or are used fictitiously.

ISBN-13: 978-0-595-40463-6 (pbk)
ISBN-13: 978-0-595-84833-1 (ebk)
ISBN-10: 0-595-40463-4 (pbk)
ISBN-10: 0-595-84833-8 (ebk)

Printed in the United States of America

The cold breeze pushed the grass sideways and exposed the bottom of the savannah vegetation. It was the kind of morning that Ndum loved to go farming and be ahead of all her neighboring workers. The birds sang familiar welcome melodies and escaped when we came closer. This was the time when lovers felt the soft warmth of their partner's skin. It was the time of the last dreams and kids will twist their faces when told to get up from bed.

My mother, Ndum was in her early sixties but looked 38.Farming was her hobby and no matter how Chia and Ngong, my elder brothers convinced her to give up farm work, she always declined. She told them she had lived by farming and no matter how little or nothing you eat, you are destined to take a shit sometime. We walked through the grass with the cold morning dew getting on our feet. It was my worst moment and I Usually conceived my silence all the way. To Ndum, it was a usual sport. I was jealous of my other brothers who were all married and no longer lived with my mother to experience all the pains of half sleep. Not only that.

I will also picture the before sleeping activity that characterized the golden union of matrimony. We passed two women on our way but could barely recognize their faces as the dark made every Image seem like shadows. It was 4.am in the morning.

My cutlass was always prepared to wage an attack on the grass. Our village, Kom, a small village in the North West Province of Cameroon depends on farming as the main economic activity. While the women specialized in growing food crop for household consumption, men concentrated on growing of cash crops for trade and exportation to other countries and industries. The main cash crop produced in Kom is coffee popularly called red beans. The men always use as a measure for wealth the number of bags of coffee their Plantations could produce. It was 8.am when I decided to get a rest because I was getting tired and hungry.

I was sweating like a maiden about to have orgasm. My white working shirt, dirt converted to brown, soaked wet from the sweat dropping off my greasy face.

'What are you doing? You haven't started working and here you are acting like a dying snake. You are nothing like your father. Your father could cut the grass till night.Ooh! This age. Children of this age are just like the tired breast of an old woman, empty of milk.' My father, Bobe Ngong was tall and athletic. His wrinkled face clearly portrayed his age. He was in his early sixties and married to 3women.My mother was the first wife and her concubines gave her much respect and honor. All three women lived in harmony like sisters. My father had three dishes of food brought to him two times in a day and three choices to make each time at a night. It was usual for the three to assemble in my mother's house, cursing my father when he felt short of meeting their needs. My father owned vast lands in different places which he shared among his wives to farm. In Kom, it is not customary for a woman to own land. The mystery is told of a woman who killed her four brothers so she could be the only surviving heir to her father's land and houses but was swallowed up by the land when she was about harvesting the proceeds of her first labor. It was a woman's destiny to occupy herself with farm and kitchen, and above all, make her husband happy.

During the coffee season, my father will employ all his able males to pick coffee in his plantations.

Every child was accustomed to the fact that they had to use their salary to pay for school. My father's only responsibility as far as our education was concerned centered on buying our books, pens and pencils. He believed that school was the Whiteman's trick to cease our lands and extort our wealth and teach us how to be their servants. My father was married to Ndum, Bih and Nain in that order. Bih, my father's second wife and a mother of three was the happiest woman in our compound because the prince of a neighboring village, Babanki, was asking for her daughter's hand in marriage. Kuo was the beauty of the village. Even though she was my half sister, I was always thinking about doing what I will not say anywhere with her. This was incest punishable with death or life exile. But Kuo's beauty washed all these thoughts away from my mind. She was as smooth as incense grease and pocessed a pair of large piercing eyes capable to turn an officer into a stripper. Her behind was carefully mapped out such that every man will think about putting a square peck into a square hole. Incest or no incest, all I knew was, I had to wash my genitals. These genitals of mine were sure dirty and stinking for it was three moons since I last washed them.

My mother also loved Kuo very much because she was hardworking. She will always help her do the farm work and the harvesting. I was resting and taking a heavy breakfast of corn-fufu and Huckleberry fried in palm oil when Kuo arrived with a hoe hung to her back like a kangaroo carrying the young.

'Why didn't you wake me up mama?'

'Well, I just figured out you needed some rest after helping your mother do farm work yesterday'. My mother replied.

'I should work hard now because I will never see any soil to till when I am finally sold to the prince'.

The two women laughed at the same time.

'So how is your mama?'

'She is fine. I left when she was preparing some Fufu and fish so you can eat when you finish working and return home.'

My face always dimpled with joy anytime I smelt the aroma from a delicious meal prepared by Bih. She was such a good cook. This time I forecasted the hot vapor coming out of the fufu and the red oil soaking the angled eye fish. It blessed the rest of my stay in the farm with joy.

I winked at Kuo and she said her usual greeting.

'How are you today brave one?

'Just missed to hear your melodious voice all day Yesterday.'

I answered.

'You always talk to your sister like she was your wife. Why don't you find yourself a woman if you think you are big enough. Come on. Finish your meal and get back to work. I know your problem. You concentrate on things that will strip you off your energy'

'Aah aah! Mama! You talk too much.'

Kuo chipped in.

Whenever Kuo was around, I was never tired of working. First so that she should know I am strong and capable of getting her on and on, second because looking at the way she poked her bottom to the air, goose pimples showered my face and a stream of current ran through my spine. I was always watchful that my mum

Should not see me gazing at my half sister lustfully. We were finally done with farm work that day and returned home with a dish of fufu and fish waiting to get our attention. We told Bih a big thank you for the lunch and retired to our tent, not bothering to put any pot on the three stoned fire.

My father's compound consisted of three huts and a modern house. The huts were for his three wives. Each woman occupied a hut where she lived in with her children. Bobe Ngong was a titled man recognized as one of the six, decorated with a red feather. This title portrayed the bravery of a warrior in battles. He had also been upgraded to quarter-head 5moons back. This title was in some places referred to as sub-chief. His main duty was to hear disputes in his jurisdiction except for sensitive issues to be directed to the palace. He was respected by all around him and his word was law. I envied my father and was always thinking of getting married to more than six women. This was because my father was served with three different bowls of food every morning and evening from his three wives. He always ate like he was about to partake in a wrestling contest. After eating, he would relax on the grass made couch and release a long fart that made the huge living room stink like a pit toilet. This always coincided with my favorite activity of taking off the dishes from my father's living room. Though he always used all the food, he was always considerate to keep a little tip for the dish clearer. This was always a little piece of meat or fish and half a loaf of fufu. I was the most senior kid and would often bully my half brothers and sisters into clearing food from my fathers table. All the other kids in the compound would sigh every time I walk up to my father's hut. 'That greedy pig will never let us have anything' they will murmur.

I could hear cries of evil masquerades not far from our compound. Evil masquerades are those that women are not permitted to see. All could identify them from their cries. They often carried around pots of fresh blood and ran across mountains and climbed very tall trees in seconds. They could disappear and appear where anyone kept harmful and dangerous voodoo. They were in charge of putting bad people on exile. The Women and female children all got into their huts and covered their faces with loincloths to make sure they did not see the evil masquerades. It was believed that if a woman saw these evil creatures, she will give birth to a child just like the masquerade.

A story was once told of a woman who heard the cries of an evil masquerade while working on the farm. This woman hid herself behind a sycamore tree and spied at the masquerade. She later on got pregnant and gave birth to a baby cloth like a masquerade. The baby later on died after three days and she never went to the chief's palace to offer sacrifices and cleanse herself as was the custom. She later on got pregnant a year after that incident and this time, she put to birth a very healthy yam. She never took chances this second time because she knew she had to do something else she would never have a human baby. She went to the chief's palace and cleansed herself with an offering of three tins of palm oil, two goats and ten layers of cloth. The next time, she gave birth to a real human baby. The female sex is most terrified of the impending danger that will befall them if they accidentally saw a forbidden masquerade.

My father came out to the yard to receive the guest into his compound. It was the custom of the village that masqueraders could not by-pass the compound of a titled man without coming in to execute the usual dancing salutation. The masqueraders could be given anything in compensation though this was not a compulsory obligation. However, my father always had a male cock around the yard for these surprise guest. His wives frowned at these occasions and tried hard to hide all cocks in their huts as soon as they heard the cries of the advancing masquerades. Little did my father know that these particular guests were headed for his compound as a final destination. These masqueraders were different. They carried along with them an elephant horn symbolizing they were messengers from the chief. This time not the chief of Kom but the chief of Babanki. Kom and Babanki were good neighbors with similar beliefs and culture. The chief of Babanki was known by all as the invisible. It was believed that no one ever saw him. What everyone saw as the chief was like a shadow representative of he who cannot be seen. It was wrong to say the chief is dead. Rather, he goes on a visit.

They danced for some minutes at the yard and came to a sudden halt.

'We bring you greetings from the invisible. He says in 10 market days, he will come to harvest from the farm you have been catering for him. He says he will come prepared to give you the things you are ready to exchange for his farm. The invisible says this farm will further strengthen the relationship between our villages hence should be fed henceforth with palm oil and goat meat. Have you heard us?'

'I have. I ask for this only. Stay and have something to tighten your bellies for you came a long way.'

'The invisible's envoys are never hungry.'

'Then tell the invisible his message has been digested and all is well.'

Soon after the messengers left, my father called out.'Biiiih'!

'Yes my husband'

Kuo's mother responded from her hut as she walked hurriedly to my father's tent. 'Is your daughter prepared for the prince?' 'Yes my husband.'

'Make sure she does no work and feed her with goat meat and palm oil so she looks healthy and beautiful before ten market days.'

'I have heard you my husband'

The time period before a wedding was the most joyous moment in any bride's life. She was usually treated like a queen and free from any kind of strenuous activity. Our people called this period the honeymoon before the honeymoon. Everything the bride said at this time was considered right and all could notice that she will be the best dressed around the village. The men considered these signs as a warning to avoid looking at these incoming brides. All Kuo knew was that she was being asked into marriage by a prince she had never seen. She had known no man in her 19 years and here she was all excited about getting married to a prince. Ever since Kuo was two, families had forecasted she will become a great beauty and started making arrangements for their sons. Luckily enough, Bih had not accepted any special gifts on Kuo's behalf and my father considered it fair for his daughters to make decisions regarding their own marriage. The dream of every woman in the village was to make children. When girls start bearing apples on their chest, their mothers will be ready to answer innocent stupid questions.

'What happens before a child is born from the stomach'?

'Why do boys have long ones and girls have flat ones?'

'Why do you leave us some nights to go sleep with papa?' were the most common questions female teenagers asked their mothers. I was cleaning my cutlass and my mother's hoe in the yard when Kuo walked up to me.

'When I will be princess, I will make you my guard'. She joked.

'I wish I had married you first so I will be your husband and not your guard.' I told Kuo looking straight into her eyes.

'But you cannot because you are my brother.'

'Who told you that? I have only one kid sister and her name is Fetse.I do not remember my mother saying I have a sister somewhere called Kuo.Look, why don't we go harvest some fruits.'

'I will be glad to' Kuo replied.

The orchard was 7minutes walk away. We were shy enough to look into each other's face. The only question she asked was my performance at school for the third term. We were a month into the long vacation and I had been promoted to the fifth form. I was considered senior elite and old people will tip me with bananas to read and translate letters from their children in distant cities. I was known around the village as 'Whiteman'. Under the mango tree, my eyes met

Kuo's and I was carried away by her looks.

'You look beautiful'

I commented looking at her very closely. She laughed in a shy manner and pretended she was concentrating on looking at the top of the tree. She picked up a dead leaf and tore it into little bits as time passed on. It was childish romance and at the same time, best romance. I looked at the opposite directions for 7 seconds and scratched my head. The most difficult thing to do was start the action. I pretended like I was beating off a bug from her shoulder while in reality, there was no bug at all. All I wanted was a thank you from her which I gained. I mimicked the reality of boldness like I had swallowed the heart of a Lion. The first step was simple. I hugged her like I was trying to console a crying mother whose son had fallen in battle. The hug felt tighter with time. I wanted her so bad that I couldn't control myself at this time. I pressed my face against her swollen breast and she was quick to response as she clung on my body like glue. I pushed her against the tree and quickly untied her loincloth. In less than no time, we were on the ground still clung to each other. I pulled up her Singlet to rest my hand on the hard and pointed nipples which I could feel piercing my chest. It was dinner time. Kuo opened her eyes like a witch surprised by daylight, got up and hurriedly put her dresses on. She had definitely come to her senses and I felt I didn't do it too good to blow her mind. She rushed back to our compound and buried herself on her bed. I was happy, shocked and guilty. It felt like I just lost a boxing fight to a man with no hands.

How I could face my half sister again, only God could tell. I decided to act like all what happened was a mere mistake. I harvested some mangoes and went up to our compound. I walked into Bih's hut carrying a basket of juicy mangoes.

'Is all well my son?'

'All is well Kuo's mother. I just harvested some mangoes and thought you should have some' I said.

'Ooh how thoughtful of you. This is the goodies of having male children who do not fear to climb a tree.

Sit down. Have you eaten my son?'

'Ohh yes. I am still heavy with the delicious meal you offered mama and me when we returned from the farm.'

The words flowed out as I tried to adjust my mental lust of thought for the just passed incident.

For a week now, Kuo seemed to be avoiding me. She did not come to our house anymore and I was scared the news of my involvement with her had leaked. I decided to wave the thought and assume it was sheer Childishness. Something inside me said I had lost a chance I will never have but I consoled myself with the thought that it was wrong for me to have anything to do with my half sister. As time passed by, I discovered myself wanting to meet Kuo and repeat the scene. This time without any mistakes. I tried to scheme a plan where I could get Kuo meet me at a secluded area but all my ideas always had loopholes. I tried to get my mother send Kuo and me to the farm so I could have a chance to do my thing.

'Mama, you've been working too much. Why not plead with Kuo so that two of us should go and finish the work while you rest home' I asked.

'That's a good idea my son. Yu've never been so eager to work. The problem is, Kuo is not allowed to do any work now because she is about to be bought. Except you will like to go alone.' My mother replied.

'I'll go some other time mama.'

I braved myself one day when the compound seemed empty. My mother had gone to visit her friend and I was praying that Kuo should be alone in her mother's hut. It seemed however that my prayers came true this time.

'What are you doing at home all by yourself' I asked.

'Just thinking about my marriage to the prince I have never seen. Is that not awful?' She asked.

'Well, a prince is always brave, handsome, rich, and loved by all the ladies. How come you have these mixed thoughts about him?'I asked while using the bed as a chair.

'If you were not my brother, I would have said I prefer to marry you.'

The words managed to escape her lips like she realized she was voicing out what was supposed to be an inner secret. She must have had a retrospective of what happened at the Orchard.

'I mean that I would have preferred to marry any person I have seen and known than someone I have never seen.' She stammered.

I was glad she had given me a cue-in.

'Beautiful maiden, it will be a bad thing if we hunt our very feelings. Let's be true to ourselves at least for once. Do not pretend you do not feel like you want to be the mother of my children. I have never met any person that thinks acts and loves like I have always wanted it to be. You are the queen of my heart. Tell me now that you do not like me and I would never ask you this again.'

She pretended she did not hear all what I said as she was busy arranging sticks to put on the fire. I had heard my father joked with his friends that our women never say yes but if they do not say no, what they mean is yes. I did not want to give Kuo an opportunity to say no. I got up, walked to the door and shut it so that only the sharp rays of sunlight could be noticed inside the smoke filled house as she had put on the fire.

'What are you doing'? She asked with a strange surprise on her face. I did not reply to this question. I just walked up to her, held her hand and pulled her to the bed.

My father had realized I was now respecting myself and behaving like a man. I would give orders to all my young ones and ensure that the compound was kept clean. I was no longer playing with little children in the yard. At nineteen, I had stripped myself off the world of virginity and being 22 now, I had slept with a couple of girls. I could feel the change inside me and the transition from a boy to a man especially as the tip of my nipple got larger and stronger. 'You need to start molding your own blocks now. It's the commencement of the dry season and you are supposed to own your place. I will give you a piece of land besides the compound so you can put up a structure of your own. You're too old to sweep your mums house. 'I saw a serious look in my father's face like I had never seen before.

'You know you are my first son and by tradition, you are supposed to be the guardian of the whole family when I'm gone. I just want you to start thinking like a man.'

It was so hot and tiring that day such that a cat could be chasing a rat and both of them walking. This was the period when children will play all day with dragon flies notorious for bringing good tidings for the dry season. It was an ideal time for swimming because the water level drops and prevents children from drowning.

I decided to go swimming in a nearby stream. Swimming was my hobby and I felt like getting inside water anytime the rays of the sun pointed sharp into the earth. I went into the neighboring compound to find out if anyone was interested to go swimming with me but the yard seemed all deserted. I decided to go alone. Approaching the stream from a distance, I saw what seemed like a female shaped naked body that looked familiar to my mind. Its familiarity transmitted an obvious message from my brain to my organs that indicated my manhood was no friend to sexy female features. It was Kuo trying to get herself dry. She seemed worn out like she had been swimming all day. I hid myself amidst the grass and peeped at the way she caressed her soft skin with the wiping cloth. When she stooped low to wipe off her feet, I saw the reality of what the working dresses always covered each time Kuo poked her her bottom to the air while working on the farm. It seemed like she was touching some soft egg and scared it will break off if she added just a little force.

'Why am I supposed to act like a stranger to this body?' I thought to myself. I got out of the grass and walked towards the stream like I did not know someone was there.

'Close your eyes!'I could hear her shout as she tried to shield the part she considered the most important in her body. I boldly walked up to her, pulled the cloth, flung it to the bush and gazed at her uncovered soft skin.

'Lets not act like we are strangers to this whole game. The first time was no mistake and I do not see why now should be.'

I tried to curdle her as I came closer to her body knowing that she wanted to do this as bad as I did.

She gripped me tight and took off my pants like she was waging a war with pants not being in the right places. I guess the right place for my pants was to be in the bush. She acted like a live chicken about to be roasted. It was a war of love. My body retaliated to her every move like it was imitating what it saw the other body doing. I felt a tight grip like I was being strangled in the fangs of a python and after 7heartbeats, the grip loosened. I continued what it seemed like pushups with my waist and my body suddenly felt like electricity had been passed through it and my energy got absorbed. It was sweet and lasted seconds. We both acted shy as we put on our dresses.

Kuo put on her dress and walked quietly home as I watched her disappear.

Ten market days had passed by and the whole compound was excited and waiting for Kuo to be bought. She was the talk of the village and everyone loved to associate with her for the last time. She was looking healthy and beautiful, probably because she was banned from working and fed with goat meat.Bih was the most proud woman in the village. When she chatted with her friends, she would not miss to talk about her daughter's marriage to the prince and how her ancestors are watching over their whole family. Women in the village became jealous and wished their daughters were in Kuo's position.

'This is sheer luck. Don't you think Neh is more beautiful than Kuo?' 'I hear Bih took her daughter to a strong witch doctor in the nearby village and was given a strong love potion which she used to charm the prince. It all stays here. You women with slippery mouths should not tell anybody I said this. 'The women laughed as they walked to the market. Bobe Ngong's compound was filled with people and color that morning. The yard had been properly cleaned and drums placed at the centre. All three women were busily cooking against the grand occasion. The Prince's father, the invisible was to be the merchant. It was tradition that parents were responsible to buy wives for their children. The invisible and his entourage were to arrive before sunset.

'Try to catch some sleep my daughter. This is going to be a long and beautiful day for you. Catch some sleep.'

Bih advised Kuo.

All three women were preparing heavy pots of fufu and shaping them into healthy calabash loaves as was the custom for this occasion. It was believed that the men are supposed to eat heavily so that they could gain energy to bring forth children. All Bobe Ngong had to do was to make his compound ready to receive guest and this time, not any kind of guest. The importance of the occasion circulated around the fact that the male fruit of Kuo's womb was to be an heir to the Babanki throne hence symbolizing an uncompromising reunion between the two villages. Rumor had circulated that the Chief of Kom will be in the occasion to see his friend buy a wife for his son.Bobe Ngong had to keep his compound ready for these august dignitaries.

A crowd of friends and relatives had begun to assemble in Bobe Ngong's yard when the sun showed signs it will set soon. The cries of palace messengers could be heard from a distance. The noise sounded closer as time narrowed. Sooner than later, the noise was at the outside of the yard and this time, heavy sounding. All stood up as was done when anything or person from the palace approached. The messenger walked in with his entourage and announced.

'His Excellency, fon Nsom of Kom, leader of a thousand clans, husband to a thousand women and father to a thousand children will be here in less than no time. This time, he comes for good news so there will be no evil masquerades. All child bearing people can still enjoy the occasion in his presence. But beware, for royalty is dangerous when not given the natural respect.'

Bobe Ngong was now wondering if there was room in his compound to take his entire guest and told me to rally the kids and we should go chair begging from the neighboring houses. The fon of Kom arrived and Bobe

Ngong received him in his living room. All his guards stood by him as he sat on the Lion skin chair and put his feet on Tiger skin all brought from the palace. In a little while, the entourage of the fon of Babanki arrived and he sat close to his friend and son on chairs decorated with animal skin brought from the Babanki palace. The drums went silent and it was time for the invisible of Babanki to speak.

'My people, our people, I have came to thank Bobe Ngong for taking care of my farm. He has been a good servant and deserves a price. I will pay him and take my farm away. He is tired and must not work again. I am armed with 30 heads of goat, 40tins of palm oil, 60 chicken and 90pieces of cloth. I think a good laborer deserves good wages. I have spoken'.

There was a heavy dance soon after that speech and the prince smiled knowing that all was going good. The dance suddenly stopped and the chief asked.

'Where is my farm?'

A group of women in a straight line, all rubbed with red cam wood from head to toe, started a line from Bih's hut. They marched slowly and silently, taking steps at the same time. They were almost half naked except for the small loin cloth that covered the front and back of the most important. Their breast was exposed to the setting sun. They were ten in number, and of the same age group all lined up before the invisible and his son. Bih now came out from her hut alone, all dressed up with goal bracelets and painted with red cam-wood, walked to the chief, knelt besides his feet as a sign of respect before asking the question.

'Which of these ten farms will you like to harvest your seeds in'

This question was directed to the prince.

'None of them, bring me my farm.' The prince replied.

Kuo came out of her mother's hut looking beautiful and terrified. Her large black eyes passed on a message of mixed feelings on her supposed most happy day. She was all dressed up with fresh leaves from head to toe and all the ten virgins sang as she came close. It was believed that the ten must be virgins but no one actually did the check.

The price had been accepted by Kuo's father hence the ceremony was to continue as was customary. It was required that the bride and the groom should acquaint themselves the first time they met by getting into an airtight room in the compound and made love till they both were satisfied and tired. During this time, the groom will also decide if he is satisfied with the performance. If not, he will claim his price and walk away. However, in most cases I had witnessed, the groom was always satisfied with the performance. It was unheard of to think the groom will be dissatisfied by what was termed the juicy first. This was because the groom was not supposed to have participated in the game before this time.Still, no one checked. Shortly before this cleansing ritual into matrimony, the bride will ask her mother what she had to do and the groom will ask his father. This was the only time they were required to know. Kuo was terrified and frightened that her husband to be will discover that she was not a virgin. This was punishable according to the village norms. Every woman was to marry being a virgin. At this moment, I left the yard and went miles away for fear that I might get into trouble if the prince discovered that his bride is not a virgin and leaked the news. Kuo's best friend, Njang, kept looking into my face the whole time I witnessed the occasion. 'I wonder if she knows anything' I thought to myself. She had a leaky mouth to say whatever she thinks and a holy stomach meant for not keeping secrets. I knew I will be screwed if she knew about this. On a second thought, maybe she was just taken away by my charms.

Inside the room, the two were naked and decided to talk like husband and wife.

'I only heard from people but I think you are most beautiful than what they say.' The prince said.

'I was scared I could be sold to an ugly prince but you are as handsome as every woman's dream. They clinked and pressed their bodies against each other so that they could feel the warmth of tightness and the smell of warm ready skin. The chemistry was already into play as the prince surrendered and attacked the elevated middle trying hard to put something into something. He was doing it from behind. The moaning from the opposite sex seemed organized and planned as it sounded uniform in pace. The soft and easily

Penetrative hole was manipulated to be firm so it may depict difficulty of penetration and a show of Virginity according to the law. Because this activity is the only struggle where one never gives up, access into the electric ocean was finally granted and the pumping aspect took precedence. Moaning was converted into actual crying as proof of pain and show of purity. How the other sex interpreted this, only him could tell for he ignored being a detective and concentrated on human dinner. Never wanting to stop, there is always a time when you cannot continue.

As the two came out of the room with the prince holding a red stained sheet as confirmation of virginity, all applauded and began singing. It was time for the prince to take his bride away since he was satisfied with his farm. The chief of Kom had something to say.

'We had fought wars in the past but our fathers say that he who wants peace must be prepared for war. This is the beginning of a union. I give the invisible a personal invitation to my sanctuary while his son is testing the rooms'

'What are we waiting for? Let's go.' The invisible replied.

Kuo's marriage was the talk of the village. All the girls and women commented on how handsome the prince looked and that he must have been charmed by Kuo. All I was happy about is the fact that the abominable never happened. We had to do a lot of cleaning around the yard the next day and build new huts for our many goats. The bride price had made my father rich. His store was packed filled with Stuff he could consume for two harvesting seasons.

My father was to give Bih's mother a greater fraction of the sale and a smaller fraction to all the other women. My father walked everywhere with a smile on his face.' My blood will be a mother of kings. My ancestors are not sleeping.' He said to himself.

It all seemed like love had rejuvenated from its hiding place when the prince met his love. All could see from his eyes that he was in love with the Kom beauty. A critic in these issues will say the look is always the same in every man's eyes when he knows he will do an exercise. Such a critic will not be very far from the truth.

'The invisible, I must let the rat out of its hiding before the cat causes disaster. It's my entire fault. I was to say this earlier but I just did not want to destabilize the peace between us and our neighbors.'

'I hear you my son. You have taken the horse to the stream, but refused to let it drink water. You are merely increasing its thirst. I am listening my son 'The prince bowed his head to the ground in a worried manner. He seemed like a bug was chopping his guts and making him feel uncomfortable. The honeymoon seemed like a dark moon. At long last, he decided to speak.

'Kuo is not a virgin'.

'How do you expect her to be when you plucked it off?'

The invisible looked perplexed and surprised. He had that look on his face anytime he wanted to order his soldiers go to war with a neighboring village.

'That's not all about it father. The worst is, she is pregnant. And not for me.'

'Hang that prostitute and feed the wolves with her remains. Why didn't you say this earlier? Do you realize the stain and humiliation you bring to royalty?

?'The chief asked angrily.

'Father, this is not about us punishing her as our custom demands. We must realize that she is not one of us and it is evident that war must accrue if we inflict harm on her. Kom people are not cowards and cannot let this lying down.' The prince tried to convince his father.

'Do not lecture the lawmaker about the do's and don'ts of the law. Just bring that prostitute out here and let's set an example to others. This is the worst scandal I have ever known about royalty hence has to be crushed instantly before it gets pregnant.'

Word had been sent to the chief of Kom about the boiling news at the Babanki palace and he sent his messengers to tell Bobe Ngong to report to his palace. It was a very solemn conversation.

'So what do you think we can do in an issue like this? We will either go to war with the people of Babanki or bury the issue and let her be punished according to their traditions and customs.Afterall she has been bought and they can now rightly term her their property.'

'Your highness, I accept that all you say is true. But don't you think that allowing the issue to be treated according to their custom will prove a weakness to the Kom people and their incapacity to stand for themselves. This is the daughter of a titled man we are talking about hence she is to be treated with respect.'

The chief of Kom contemplated for a while and then finally said.' We have three days to make a decision. Think over this carefully and send me word tomorrow. Try to find out who is responsible for the current pregnancy and we can try an alternative of punishing the culprits under our own customs. I am waiting to hear from you tomorrow' Bobe Ngong had never been worried in his life like he was at the moment. He called me into his living room and ordered me to have a sit. He tried to inquire from me if there was any boy who was always with Kuo. At first, he felt like I was not supposed to know about all the stuff but finally gave it up.

'Look son, I must tell you this. Your sister is now a disgrace to the Kom people and this might cause war. She is pregnant. All I will like to know from you is that you tell me who is responsible for this Pregnancy. I was speechless for a while before giving an answer.

'I have no idea about this father.'

It was now evident that some terrible news was about to leak. I started thinking about an escape up North to Oku. An idea came to my mind. I told my father the next morning that it will be good I go to the palace at Babanki and find out about my half sister's situation. I would pretend I was bringing the rest of her stuff she left home. Then I would personally talk with her and find out the situation at hand. My father accepted and praised me for thinking like a man. My bag was filled with food the next morning because my journey was long. Anytime I was about to trek on an errand by my father, Ndum will fill up my food bag to the brim and say a special prayer on my behalf. The part I enjoyed the most was when she said that if my foot hit against a stone, the stone should break off and my foot should remain healthy.

The protocol at the palace gate in Babanki was Strict and strong. I had to present my father's red feather at the magical entrance before I could be granted access into the palace. The entrance was well noted for filtration. Anyone getting into the palace with any form of magical power was chased by the palace spirits at the gate. I asked to see Kuo and was told to wait for a while. The guards took the message to the prince and presented my red feather.

'Identify yourself' the prince commanded while walking into the waiting room.

'Kuo is my half sister and I have come to pay her a visit'

'Is there any problem?' the prince asked.

'No' I replied.

The prince got inside and Kuo came out after a while. She was full of grief like she had lost a close relative. I talked to her about my plan and proposal to handle the situation.

We reached a decision before I could see that expensive and beautiful smile on her face. It was time to go and I was thinking about what to tell my father after scheming up my own personal agenda.

In the Babanki palace, the dispute between the prince and his wife had created a tensed and confused atmosphere. Kuo had denied all charges that she had been having an affair with another man order than the prince. Although the palace magician had cast lots and told the prince that his wife was pregnant, Kuo had denied all the charges. She had said that it must be a mystery if true but the prince affirmed that she was not a virgin on her wedding ceremony. The prince said he did not face any difficulty to penetrate but pretended all was right because he didn't know she was pregnant.

'I know what it feels like. I had slept with many virgins before so do not try to fool me.' The prince argued.

'Even if I'm not, you are not to be angry because I am not the first woman yu've slept with' Kuo contradicted.

'Shut up!' the prince retorted angrily.

My father sent word to the chief that he was unable to know who actually was responsible for the pregnancy and that he had sent me to Bih but I was not able to come home with any favorable answer. It was certain that a great war was in the making. My father was very depressed and could not even eat up all his usual three bowls of food for lunch. He called me to his living room that day after sunset and told me all about the situation at hand.

'This is a terrible thing my son. Your sister has brought disgrace upon this family and to the Kom people as a whole. What is your idea of what can be done?' My father asked feeling depressed. This was the first time my father ever asked my opinion on a trivial issue.

'Father I think we should not let Kuo die because no matter what happens, she is our blood.'

According to History, the last war fought between the people of kom and Babanki was 113 years back. The main cause of this war was land dispute. Yet, there is about to be another war over an issue which on the contrary was speculated to bring lasting peace. I had been thinking that the chief of Kom will not afford to loose the lives of his warriors because of some prostitute. My plan was ripe. It was midnight when I waited outside the Babanki Palace besides a huge oak tree. I was worn out after many hours of trekking but ready to take Bih to my friend's house in Oku. Oku is a big village in the North of Kom, notorious for its great lake which was considered a centre and market place for witchcraft. Tosam migrated to Oku when he turned 17 and often came to Kom for visits or special occasions. His father was Kom and his mother, from Oku.Ever since Tosam lost his father; his paternal relatives took occupancy of their compound and tortured his mother so much so that she decided to migrate to Oku. It was tradition that every widow is treated badly because she did not take proper care of her husband hence causing his death. Women often loved to die before their husbands because they knew their life will be miserable after their husband's death. Tosam had a step mother but she stayed in Kom because she had no where else to go.

It was a carefully planned arrangement first to Oku where I told Tosam about the whole situation and how I planned to escape with Bih and hide in his little hut.

It was a long wait such that I was almost contemplating to leave for fear that the plan must have been foretold by fortune tellers of the Babanki palace whose only job was spiritism and fortune telling. I heard a sound like the grass was tearing apart and finally released a figure of a man carrying a spear. I hid behind the huge oak tree knowing this was all a life and death issue. I prayed to my ancestor not to make this happen. I listened to a series of noisy and silent steps which revealed immediately to my senses that two people were drawing closer.

'I do not see anyone here'. I heard a male voice say.

'Lets wait. He will be here in a moment' the voice Sounded like one I was quite familiar with. I knew at once that it was Kuo.I came out of my hiding.

'You need to go now before the other guards and the prince notice your absence'

'Thank you'.Kuo said to the guard and we left immediately without offering a word to each other till we had trekked about half a mile. Kuo had told the guard that she was going to compensate him with 10 goats if he helped her escape. The guard was withholding all of Kuo's clothes except some few pieces of cloth she took along. The agreement was that if Kuo didn't come back, he will own the clothes.

'Is all going as planned?' Kuo broke the silence.

'Yes' was my answer.

My mind was preoccupied with nasty thoughts about taking a moment and relaxing in the bush before I continue to my final destination. However, I had one major worry. I did not tell Tosam all what actually happened. He was ignorant about the fact that I was the architect of Kuo's pregnancy. He had accepted that we hide in his hut just because he was interested in Kuo. A number of times when he was on one of his visits to Kom, he had pleaded with me to match him up with my sister but for jealousy sake, I had always said that I had talked to Kuo but she was not interested about all those kind of stuff.

My father had realized I had not taken the goats up the hill in the morning. He had sent for me when it was almost sunrise and Ndum said she too was worried because I did not sleep at home that night. My father was immediately alerted and the first issue that came to his mind was that the people of Babanki had kidnapped me so that my whole village should feel the impact and fear going to war because Kuo and me will both be killed. He sent word to the chief immediately that I was missing. The chief sent word back that my father should came in person so that they could discuss on the next plan of action.

'In this kind of situation, what we usually do is beat up an agreement with our rivals because war will mean a great loss to you in particular and to the Kom people as a whole' the chief said.' What I was thinking is that we should send word to the chief of Babanki and give a proposal of either land compensation or food and animals' the chief continued.

My father thought for a while and said.

'Your words have always been wisdom great one. It will be helpful if we proceed with the plan immediately.' My father responded feeling happy and released. It's never been easy to walk incognito. Kuo and I tried not to be noticed by anyone on the way. News circulated around the village like smoke from a huge fire. It was no doubt that the Invisible of Babanki could trace our destination if anyone informed him that we passed north towards Oku. Guards would be running after us like they were not destined to get tired.

The chief of Kom looked to the ceiling in confusion. It was hard to believe what the messenger had said. He could not even think of the possibility of how it all happened. Why did the guards not realize this? It all seemed to him like a great confusion and a manipulative pretext of war. Kuo had escaped and the invisible sends war threats because he knows that the Kom magicians had penetrated the palace and taken her away. This situation was going off hand. When my father heard this, he cursed his ancestors for sleeping in daylight. He asked himself the question.

'Where might they be?' My father could never believe my actions and it all sounded to him like we were in some kind of trouble. He knew it was no doubt that trouble was inevitable. He had been commanded by the chief to prepare his regiments for war. The village spokesman passed the announcement around every compound that every able male capable of making a woman pregnant should assemble in my father's compound for a brief training for war. Young people were excited at this time because they had always wanted to fight wars. They were to be trained by my father who is a war lord.

They planned to leave the village that night so that they will embark a surprise attack on the Babanki people before the news of war preparation leaked.

Something deep inside was telling me this is not the right thing to do. Kuo was happy being besides me with no threats of death. She was ready to keep my baby and said we could spend the rest of our lives in Oku. To me, it sounded like a very odd idea. I thought about my family back home in Kom and how everyone could be worried not knowing where on earth I was. Tosam had finally discovered the emotional attraction between Kuo and I and was very cold to us thence. He had been thinking that this was his only opportunity to bed sport with Kuo. The first day, he played a nice guy and brought down all the meat from his smoked ceiling and asked Kuo to cook as much as she loved to. Meat was always the issue. A woman could marry a sterile cripple, provided he had enough meat to smoke in his ceiling. I knew for sure that it was no longer a season to play around. It was time to go.

'How could you do that to your own sister' Tosam asked surprised at my action.

'Well I like her and besides, she is not my blood sister. If we perform the rituals and give sacrifices to the gods of incest, we can be allowed to marry and live normal lives like any other person.'

The Kom warriors had surrounded the Babanki palace. It was about 3 O'clock in the morning when all warriors waited for the war lord to give the order. The palace magician was ahead to alert the war lord that there wasn't any evil spirit on the way and it was time to attack. He had said an hour ago that it was not yet time to attack and that the warriors should hold their patience. He was listening to the air like he felt something coming. The warriors had waited for over an hour and were now impatient. Kuo and I walked through the bush and the closer we were to the Babanki Palace, the more frightened we became. I had decided to brave the situation like a man even if it could cause me my own life. It was obvious that we were to be punished for escaping but we had no where else to go.

The warriors were alerted with the sound of people coming behind just to be discouraged that it was me and my sister. They however did not came out of their hiding because the feared it could be mere shadows that the Babanki magicians were using to divert our attention. The Kom magician appeared before Kuo and I like a wind and asked us where we are coming from. I was filled with shock and Kuo collapsed when an image appeared before her. The war battalion quickly assembled and tried to reach a quick plan. The Kom magician said he will take the news to the chief of Kom and be back before the cock crow. This was a distance of 7 hours trek to the Kom palace but here was a magician saying he will cover this distance in less than 30 minutes before it was 4a.m when the cock had to crow.Kuo and I were placed in the middle of the circle and questioned silently. I unleashed the truth of my affair with Kuo and told all the people that Kuo's pregnancy was my responsibility. I told my father that I would like to do all the necessary rituals and marry her. After all, the ritual was inevitable because what had been done had been done.

'Do not worry yourself my son. Let's just wait and listen to what the chief will say before we can make a concrete decision on this issue.' I was surprised when my father released these words because I thought he would be mad and curse me for bringing shame to his family. The chief and the magician miraculously appeared from a distance and in less than no time; they were at the centre of the scene. It seemed to me like the chief was hiding in a nearby bush and the magician just fished him out to the scene. The three talked for a while before the cock had to crow. They had reached a decision. They walked like in a procession to the Babanki palace just after the cockcrow. The chief of Babanki came out with his own warriors behind him. The warriors in Babanki were not many to stand a fight. The invisible stood at the other side of the palace gate and spoke out.

'If you came for war, then do not feel that you take us unprepared for you are sorrounded.But if you came for peace, then you are welcome and can walk into my palace.'

'We came for peace' the chief of Kom replied as they all walked into the palace. A huge fire was made at the palace centre to welcome the guest.

'I have a proposal to make. Let's not kill our people by going to war. We can return your bride price and make any necessary ammenments.Lets end this conflict and continue our ever existing friendship. It is useless for salt and meat to be at loggerheads with each other because they need each other to taste good. Let me hear what the invisible has to say.' The chief of Babanki contemplated for a while but it seemed finally that he had decided on what to say.

'I accept your terms but will not accept that you give back the bride price. I ask for a dance to be held in your village in two market days. Let all the virgins of your village make it to that dance and my son will choose for himself a wife among your people.' I accept, the chief of Kom responded.

My father sent for me and asked me to eat with him.

News of my affair with Kuo had circulated around the village and it seemed like the worst scandal ever conceived. 'There is something I must tell you.' My father said. I knew for once that he was about to disown me. I just considered this meal the last super.'Kuo is not my daughter. Her mother was pregnant with her before she was bought into my family. There is no need for any ritual because she is not my blood. You can go ahead and buy her if you like.' The words seemed to me like they came from an abstract world. I struggled to digest what I heard and tried to hide my feelings. I just couldn't. I smiled but remained silent.

'I will give you land to farm on and start a life of your own. You can build yourself a hut. Do not labor yourself on building a compound for you are my heir and I am getting old. All what I own will eventually be yours. Just promise to take care of all what I leave behind' I managed to hold the excitement and answered.

'I will father. But I do not want you to die.'

'I do not want to die either. I just want you to promise me that in case something happens, you will take care of the family.'

It was the grand village dance and the prince had to choose his bride. All the young girls in the village were dressed in their best outfits and looking charming. Every girl wanted to be the prince's favorite as they cursed Kuo for missing a life happy opportunity. The dance was filled with color as every female tried to be beautiful and noticed. The prince had not picked his lady yet.

'Father, I think I should take Kuo with her pregnancy because I really like that girl. None of these girls move me like she does.'

'Look carefully my son. You must find your match amidst this whole bunch of beauties' the invisible advised his son. The prince made up his mind that he will take Kuo back to the palace and the invisible accepted his son's choice. The prince stood up to make a speech.

'It has been a wonderful dance. I will take my woman back to the palace. Our honeymoon was not yet over. I like her and will accept her pregnancy. Let her came to me if she thinks what I have said is right.' Kuo was not dressed and prepared for this occasion like the other girls were. She was actually surprised when the prince said this. My father was confused and at the same time happy that the prince was ready to accept

Kuo back into the palace. He gazed at me and the message I read from his eyes said

'Do not even try to disrupt this happiness'. I felt a particular joy inside me when the prince said he will accept the pregnancy. All I wanted was for Kuo to be happy. I realized at this time that I did not really love her after all because I was not jealous. I just loved to feel her body juice lighten my flesh. My father had something to say 'I know you all are thinking about my son making my daughter pregnant. This is supposed to be incest and they are supposed to be cleansed. I am happy to say that Kuo is not my blood daughter. I won't go into details. Just want you to know that there is no problem after all. The whole area was silent as my father concluded. Everyone looked at me trying to deduce my facial reaction. I hid my face to the ground as if shy and in prayer 'Thank you prince for uplifting the burden and shame upon me and my family. I can now find my true love because I did not truly love Kuo after all. Njang looked into my eyes and smiled. I felt like she was the chosen one. A huge smile crossed my face when I thought about not only flirting with her but also making her mine.

978-0-595-40463-6
0-595-40463-4